CHINESE NEW YEAR

a **MR. MEN**™ **LITTLE MISS**™ book

originated by Roger Hargreaves

Written and illustrated by Adam Hargreaves

Grosset & Dunlap

Little Miss Neat was very busy cleaning her house.

It was the day before Chinese New Year, and this was Little Miss Neat's favorite day of the year.

Spring-cleaning day!

She wanted to clean away all of last year's bad luck.

And, as we all know, Little Miss Neat loves to clean.

She even vacuumed the walls!

There were lots of things she had to do to make sure that her New Year's party went well.

Little Miss Neat had asked her friends to help her decorate her house for the New Year.

Little Miss Sunshine set out flowers.

Little Miss Lucky hung paper cutouts for happiness.

And Mr. Tall hung lanterns.

High up in the tree.

Very high up!

And then Mr. Wrong hung the lucky Chinese poems . . . upside down!

Which turned out to be the right way up because it was lucky to hang them upside down.

It's not often that Mr. Wrong gets something right.

Red is the good-luck color for the Chinese New Year, and Little Miss Neat made sure there was a lot of red in her house.

For extra luck, Mr. Silly got out the red paint.

And painted the doormat!

Little Miss Neat did not think this was very lucky.

What a mess!

Little Miss Splendid used the coming celebration as an excuse to buy a new hat.

A truly splendid red hat!

Everyone was excited when they arrived for New Year's Eve dinner that evening.

It was an enormous feast.

Mr. Greedy smiled and started munching.

He ate the beef and the pork and the vegetables and the chicken.

He ate everything.

He even ate all the fish!

Little Miss Neat was not very happy, because it was a Chinese New Year's tradition to leave some of the fish.

Greedy old Mr. Greedy!

Each New Year was represented by a different animal.

There were twelve animals, and Little Miss Naughty was born in the Year of the Rat.

After dinner, she crept up behind Little Miss Shy wearing a rat mask.

Little Miss Shy screamed and leaped into the air.

She was so embarrassed she turned bright red.

"You'll have luck all year," laughed
Little Miss Lucky.

The next day, Mr. Muddle led the dragon dance down the street.

Unfortunately, what followed Mr. Muddle's lead . . .

After this, everyone gave each other a red envelope with a gift of money inside.

Well, not quite everyone.

Every time Mr. Mean tried to give away his red envelope, he just could not quite bring himself to do it.

He truly is the meanest!

On the last day of the New Year celebrations, Little Miss Neat invited all her friends to visit her garden. She had bought a lot of fireworks because the loud bangs would chase away all the bad luck for the next year.

But she had not counted on Mr. Bump.

Mr. Bump is not a very lucky person.

In fact, he is not lucky at all.

While he was carrying the fireworks, he somehow managed to trip, and he dropped all the fireworks into the pond.

"Oh no!" cried Little Miss Neat. "How are we going to chase away next year's bad luck?"

"HELLO!" boomed a very loud voice, suddenly.

It was Mr. Noisy.

And, as you know, Mr. Noisy is very loud.

More than loud enough to scare away any bad luck.

He happens to be loud *and* red!

"Now, that's what I call lucky," said Little Miss Lucky.